FROSTY the SNOWMAN

Retold by Carol North
Illustrated by Terri Super

A GOLDEN BOOK • NEW YORK
Western Publishing Company, Inc., Racine, Wisconsin 53404

© Warner/Chappell Music 1990. All rights reserved. Printed in the U.S.A. No part of this book may be reproduced or copied in any form without written permission from the publisher. GOLDEN, GOLDEN & DESIGN, GOLDENCRAFT, A GOLDEN BOOK, and A GOLDEN SUPER SHAPE BOOK are registered trademarks of Western Publishing Company, Inc. ISBN: 0-307-10039-1/ISBN: 0-307-61039-X (lib. bdg.)
A B C D E F G H I J K L M

Once upon a time there was a snowman
named Frosty.

The children loved to play with Frosty. They formed a ring and danced around him.

"I wish Frosty could talk to us," said one of the children.

One day the children brought an old silk hat for Frosty to wear. As soon as they put it on his head, a magical thing happened. Frosty began to sing and dance.

Frosty the snowman was alive!

The children were so happy. They came to play with Frosty every day.

Frosty and the children went ice skating together. Round and round they skated on the frozen pond.

Once Frosty slipped and fell—*kerplunk!* But he just smiled his magical smile and jumped right back up.

Another time Frosty and the children all piled
on a sled and went sledding.
"Weeeeeeeeee," said Frosty. "Look at us go!"

One day Frosty said to the children, "Would you take me to town? I've never been in a town." They all skipped along, smiling and laughing all the way.

Frosty looked in a pet shop window. He even pressed his nose up against the glass to get a closer look.

When Frosty and the children got to the bakeshop, Frosty looked at the muffins in the window. "Can we go inside and get a muffin?" he asked. "I've never had a muffin."

But when they went inside the shop, Frosty
began to melt! "Oh, I must go back outside,"
said Frosty.

Frosty ate his muffin sitting on a bench, with
the children gathered around.

At the end of the day Frosty smiled his magical smile and said, "We've had such a good time today. I'll never forget it." He had a special gleam in his eyes.

Soon the days got warmer and the snow began to melt.

When the children came out to play one really sunny day, they couldn't find Frosty. They looked everywhere. Finally they went to the bakeshop, and there on the bench outside was a note. It was from Frosty.

And the children didn't cry. They knew that
Frosty would come back. They could picture his
magical smile and feel his warm heart.
   Can you?

Thumpety thump thump, thumpety thump thump,
Look at Frosty go.
Thumpety thump thump, thumpety thump thump,
Over the hills of snow.